A Tale of Two Cities

Charles Dickens

HAR-ANAND
PUBLICATIONS PVT LTD

HAR-ANAND PUBLICATIONS PVT LTD

E-49/3, Okhla Industrial Area, Phase-II, New Delhi-110020
Tel.: 41603490
E-mail: info@haranandbooks.com / haranand@rediffmail.com
Shop online at: www.haranandbooks.com

Published by Ashok Gosain and Ashish Gosain for
Har-Anand Publications Pvt Ltd

Printed in India by Hi-Tech Graphics

Principal Characters

Dr. Manette : A doctor who is imprisoned for eighteen years

Lucie Manette : Dr. Manette's daughter

Charles Darnay : A Frenchman who lives in England

Sidney Carton : A lawyer

Mr. Jarvis Lorry : A friend of the Manette family

Miss Pross : Lucie Manette's companion

Monsieur Defarge : The owner of a wine-shop in Paris

Madame Defarge : Monsieur Defarge's wife

Contents

ONE

Recalled to Life

In the year 1775, there was a king and queen on the throne of England and a king and queen on the throne of France. It was a time of turmoil in both the countries.

In France, a youth could have his hands cut off because he had not knelt down in honour of a procession of monks.

In England too, there was scarcely more order. Daring burglaries by armed men took place every night.

On one Friday night, late in November, a coach carrying the mail from Dover was slowly moving uphill. The passengers, coachman and guard were walking by its side because the hill was very steep.

The passengers were wrapped in heavy clothes. Travellers in those days did not like to be recognised as anyone on the streets might be a robber or in league with robbers. They suspected everyone.

The coach finally reached the summit of the hill. The guard opened the coach door to let the passengers in.

"Joe!" cried the coachman in a warning voice, "Listen."

They heard the sound of a horse.

The guard told the passengers to hurry up and get into the coach. They all listened and looked back.

The hearts of the passengers beat loud enough to be heard.

The sound of a horse came up the hill.

"You there," said the guard, "Stand! I shall shoot!"

"Is that the Dover mail?" a man's voice called.

"Why do you want to know?"

"I want Mr. Jarvis Lorry."

"What is the matter?" asked a passenger getting down from the coach, "Is that Jerry?"

"Yes, Mr. Lorry."

"I know this messenger, guard," said Mr. Lorry. "He may come closer; there's nothing wrong."

The rider handed the passenger a small folded paper.

"I belong to Tellson's Bank in London," said Mr. Lorry to the guard. "I am going to Paris on business. May I read this."

"Be quick, sir," said the guard.

"Wait at Dover for Mam' selle," said the message.

"Jerry, say that my answer is, *Recalled to Life*," said Mr. Lorry.

"Good night." The passenger then got into the coach.

The coach moved on again and Jerry was left alone in the darkness.

"Recalled to life," he said to his horse. "That's a strange message."

The passenger in the coach sat dozing, his thoughts wandering. He saw on his way, someone being dug out of a grave. He saw the face of the buried person. A man of forty five years with sunken cheeks and an emaciated figure. His hair was prematurely white. The passenger asked the man —

"How long have you been buried?"

"Almost eighteen years," said the man.

"You know that you have been recalled to life. I hope you care to live."

"I can't say."

The words were still in his mind as if they had just been spoken.

When the mail reached Dover, Mr. Lorry got down at the Royal George Hotel. He wanted a bedroom.

After changing Mr. Lorry went to the coffee-room. The wraps of clothes had been replaced by a brown suit. A gentleman of sixty, he sat alone in the coffee-room.

"I wish to have a room for a young lady who may come here at any time today," he said to the waiter.

The young lady whose arrival Mr. Lorry awaited arrived after dinner. The waiter came in to announce that Miss Manette had arrived from London.

Miss Manette was a young lady of not more than seventeen. She was short and slight with a pretty figure. Her hair was golden and eyes a deep blue. On arrival Miss Manette looked inquiringly at Mr. Lorry.

Mr. Lorry saw a vivid likeness of a child, whom he had held in his arms, in her. He bowed to Miss Manette.

"Take a seat sir," said Miss Manette in a clear and pleasant voice. "I received a letter from the bank informing me of some new discovery about the property of my father who died so long ago."

"Miss Manette," said Mr. Lorry. "I will relate a story to you."

"Story!"

"Yes. It's the story of a French gentleman. He was a doctor of repute in Paris. I was working in our branch in France at that time—twenty years ago. He married an English lady and I was the trustee of his affairs."

"But this is my father's story," said Miss Manette. "My mother died two years after my father's death. Was it you who brought me to England? I am almost sure it was you."

Mr. Lorry took her hand and said, "Miss Manette, it was I. But, your father had not died."

Miss Manette caught his wrist with a start.

"Pray control yourself," said Mr. Lorry. "Monsieur Manette had not died but suddenly and silently disappeared. His wife suffered so much that she did not want you to share her pain. So she told you that your father was dead."

Miss Manette fell on her knees and said, "O dear sir, tell me the whole truth."

"Your mother left you as a child," said Mr. Lorry, "to grow to be a beautiful and happy child. Your parents had no great possessions so the new discovery is not of money or property. But, your father has been found. He is alive. He has greatly changed, almost a wreck.

He has been taken to the house of an old servant in Paris. We are going there to identify him. You have to restore him to life."

A shiver ran through her frame.

"One more thing," said Mr. Lorry patting her hand. "He has been found under another name. His own name has been long forgotten or concealed. It would be dangerous to make any inquiries for a while. We must bring him from France to the safety of England. Avoid talking about this matter. I carry not a scrap of writing referring to it."

A wild looking woman came rushing into the room and pushed Mr. Lorry away. "Couldn't you tell her what you had to without frightening her to death?" she asked indignantly.

"I hope that you will accompany Miss Manette to France," said Mr. Lorry.

Far away in Paris, a large cask of wine had dropped and broken in a street, while it was being taken out of a cart. All the people had left their work to drink the wine. Some men knelt down and tried to scoop the wine in their hands. Others, tried to collect it in broken mugs or even handkerchiefs. Some tried to lick the broken pieces of the cask.

The wine had spilt on the narrow street in the suburb of Saint Antoine. A tall man dipped his finger in the muddy wine and wrote on the wall—Blood.

A time was to come when blood would be spilt on the street stones.

Hunger was prevalent everywhere. A wine-shop in the corner of the street looked better than most of the others. The wine-shopkeeper Defarge was a man of thirty. He looked like a man of strong resolution. His wife, Madame Defarge, sat in the shop behind the counter. She was a stout woman with a watchful eye. She looked as if she did not often make mistakes and had a strong character. As she sat knitting she lifted her eyebrows and gave a short cough. This suggested to her husband that he should attend the new customer who had dropped in at the shop.

The wine-shopkeeper's eyes rested for a while on an elderly gentleman and a young lady, who were seated in a corner. He pretended not to notice the two strangers. He went to attend the three customers who were drinking at the counter.

"How are things, Jacques?" said one of them to Monsieur Defarge. "Has the spilt wine been swallowed?"

"Every drop," said Monsieur Defarge.

It is not often," said the second of the three customers, "that these miserable people get to taste wine."

"It is true," said Monsieur Defarge.

The last of the three put down his glass and said, "They live a hard life, Jacques."

"You are right," responded Monsieur Defarge.

They paid for their wine and left the place. The elderly gentleman now went upto him. They spoke quietly for a minute and then the gentleman called the young girl to join them. Madame Defarge kept on knitting.

Mr. Jarvis Lorry and Miss Manette followed Monsieur Defarge into a doorway which led to a gloomy and stinking little black courtyard.

Monsieur Defarge bent down on one knee to kiss the hand of the child of his old master. He then led them to a gloomy stairway.

"It is very high," he said. "Better climb slowly."

"Is he alone?" asked Mr. Lorry

"Yes," said Monsieur Defarge. "It's his desire to be alone and it is also a necessity. After they found me, they wanted to know if I would take him. I took him at my peril and had to be discreet. He is greatly changed."

They climbed the staircase slowly. Each room of the high building threw the refuse out of the window or left it on its landing. Mr. Lorry stopped twice to rest. Foul vapours filled the atmosphere.

At last, they reached the top of the staircase. The wine-shopkeeper took out a key from the pocket of his coat.

"The door is locked?" said Mr. Lorry, surprised.

"Yes," said Monsieur Defarge. "He has lived so long, locked up that he would be frightened—harm himself—if his door was left open."

This dialogue was held in a low whisper so the young lady did not hear it. She trembled with anxiety and terror.

The three men who shared the name 'Jacques' stood at the top of the staircase. Monsieur Defarge asked them to leave.

"I show Monsieur Manette to a chosen few," said Monsieur Defarge. "Their name is the same as mine—Jacques."

He unlocked the door and beckoned them to enter.

"I am afraid," said the girl.

"Of what?" asked Mr. Lorry.

"Of my father," replied Miss Manette.

Mr. Lorry held her hand and led her into the room.

The room was a store for firewood. It was dim and dark. A white-haired man sat on a low bench, stooping forward busy making shoes.

"Good-day!" said Monsieur Defarge to him.

The white head raised for a moment and a very faint voice responded, "Good-day!"

The voice was faint due to solitude and disuse. It was the voice of a hopeless and lost creature. An unfinished shoe lay upon his lap, common tools and scraps of leather were at his feet and on the bench. He had a white beard, raggedly cut, but not very long. He had a hollow face and very bright eyes. He wore faded and tattered clothes. He did not look at the people in the room.

"You have a visitor," said Monsieur Defarge.

"Show him that shoe you are making."

Mr. Lorry took the shoe in his hand.

"Tell Monsieur what kind of shoe it is." There was a long pause.

"What did you say?" asked the shoemaker.

Monsieur Defarge repeated his words.

"It's a lady's walking shoes," said Monsieur Manette with a touch of pride.

"And what is the maker's name?" said Defarge.

"One Hundred and Five, North Tower," said Monsieur Manette. He bent to work again.

"You are not a shoemaker by trade?" asked Mr. Lorry.

"No, I am not a shoemaker by trade," said Monsieur Manette. "I taught myself. I asked for permission to teach myself, and I got it with much difficulty after a long time. I have made shoes ever since—"

"Monsieur Manette," said Mr. Lorry. "Do you remember nothing of me?"

The shoe-maker looked at the questioner.

Mr. Lorry laid his hand upon Defarge's arm, "Do you remember nothing of this man?"

Monsieur Manette looked at Mr. Lorry and at Defarge in turns. His eyes were gloomy and abstract.

"Yes," he said at last, "I knew this face a long time ago." He then stared at the girl with a fearful look. Tears streamed down her face.

"You are not the jailor's daughter?" he asked.

She sighed and said, "No."

"Who are you?"

She sat down on the bench beside him and laid her hand on his arm.

Monsieur Manette laid down his work and put his hand to his neck. He took off a blackened string with a scrap of folded rag attached to it. He opened it

18

carefully and put it on his knee. It contained a little quantity of golden hair.

He took her hair and looked closely at it. "It is the same," he said. "How can it be! She laid her head upon my shoulder that night when I was summoned out. She feared my going. When I was brought to the North Tower they found those upon my sleeve. "Leave them for me. They can never help me to escape in body though they may in spirit. Those were the words I said. I remember them very well."

He said these words coherently though slowly.

"Was it you?" he asked. "No, no, no; you are too young. What is your name, my gentle angel?"

"You shall know my name and who my parents are," said Miss Manette. She held him close round the neck, and rocked him like a child. "I have come to take you to England to be at peace and to rest."

He rested his head upon her arm.

"Can we leave Paris at once?" she asked Mr. Lorry, who was also blowing his nose.

"But, is he fit for the journey?" asked Mr. Lorry.

"He cannot remain in this city that has been so dreadful to him," she said.

Monsieur Defarge agreed with her and offered to make arrangements for a carriage.

Miss Manette wanted to stay with her father alone. The other two men left reluctantly. They were not in favour of leaving together. But, the travelling papers had to be prepared and so they had to leave.

Then, as it got dark, Mr. Lorry and Monsieur Defarge returned having made all the arrangements.

They helped Monsieur Manette. He looked scared and confused. He occasionally clasped his head in his hand and turned to his daughter. He readily held her hand in his own.

They led him down the stairs into a carriage. He asked for his shoe-making tools and the unfinished shoes. Madame Defarge immediately brought them to him.

They rode through the night. Mr. Lorry sat opposite the man who had been buried for eighteen years. He had now been recalled to life.

Two

Five Years Later

Five years later.... on a March morning in the year, 1780, the chief clerk of the Tellson's Bank sent Jerry a messenger with a message for Mr. Lorry. The case being tried was of treason. If found guilty, the prisoner would be hanged.

Jerry saw Mr. Lorry seated at a table with the defence lawyer Mr. Stryver. A counsel sat next to them with a pile of papers before him. He seemed indifferent to the surroundings and sat with his hands in his pockets with his whole attention on the ceiling of the court.

The prisoner Charles Darnay was a young man of about twenty five. He was good looking and looked self-possessed but stood quietly and bowed before the judge.

Everybody present in the court, stared at the prisoner. They mentally hanged him. Darnay had pleaded 'not guilty' to the charge of treason. He was accused of assisting the French King Lewis in his war against the King of England.

The accused was quiet and attentive and watched the proceeding with a grave interest. He turned his

22

face to the left of the court. A young lady sat her father. Her hands were drawn through his Her face showed pity for him.

Jerry asked the people about him, "Who are they?"

"Witnesses against the prisoner," was the reply he got.

The Attorney-General informed the jury that the prisoner had been passing between France and England on a secret business for some years. Documents had been found in the prisoner's home showing the lists and disposition of His Majesty's forces.

The prisoner's own friend John Barsad and his servant Roger Cly had given evidence against him. They had decided to betray their friend and master when they came to know of his treason.

When the Attorney-General concluded his speech the prisoner was considered as good as dead.

The defence counsel begged to ask a few questions. He first questioned John Barsad. He was found to be in debt. He had also been to the debtor's prison a few times. He had been found cheating at gambling. He had borrowed money from the prisoner but was in no position of returning it. He himself had got the military lists and his sole purpose was to entrap him in a false case.

The servant, Roger Cly had been working for the prisoner for four years. He had seen the lists with the prisoner and had also seen him show these lists to a French gentlemen. Roger Cly said his only motive to give evidence against his master was patriotism.

ral then called Mr. Jarvis Lorry
He was asked to testify if he had
n his travels between England and
reluctantly admitted that he had
r on the ship, which was returning
re than once.

M...   tte was called next. She said that she
had met the prisoner along with Mr. Lorry on the ship.
She turned lovingly towards the prisoner and said,
"When the prisoner came on board, he noticed that my
father was very weak and tired. He helped me make
him comfortable and shelter him from the weather."

"Did he come on board alone?"

"No," said Miss Manette, "there were two French
gentlemen with him."

"Did they exchange any papers?"

"Some papers had been handed about among them,
but I don't know what papers," said Miss Manette. "I
only know that he was very kind and I do not want to
repay him by doing him harm. He told me that he was
travelling under an assumed name as his business was
of a delicate nature. It required him to travel between
France and England very often."

Her face was painfully anxious and she watched
the effect of her evidence on the judge.

The Attorney-General then called Doctor Manette.
"Have you ever seen the prisoner before?"

"Once," said Dr. Manette, "when he visited us at
home in London. I don't remember seeing him on the
ship as I had been newly released from prison and my
mind was blank.

Mr. Attorney-General then called other witnesses who identified the prisoner to be the one who had travelled between France and England.

The gentleman who had all this time been looking at the ceiling of the court, wrote a word or two on a little piece of paper. He tossed it to Mr. Stryver. Opening this piece of paper, the defence counsel asked a witness, "Are you quite sure that it was the prisoner?"

The witness was quite sure.

"Did you ever see anybody who looked very much like the prisoner?" said Mr. Stryver.

"Not that I could be mistaken," said the witness.

"Look carefully at that gentleman there," said the defence counsel pointing to the man who had tossed the paper, "and then look at the prisoner. What do you say? Are they not very much like each other?"

Not only the witness, but everybody present was surprised to see how alike the two looked. Mr. Stryver asked the court if his friend Mr. Carton would also be tried for treason. He then concluded that Barsad and Cly were partners. They were traitors and the prisoner was their victim. He had to travel to France because of family affairs. The evidence against him had been warped.

The jury left to consider the case. The trial had lasted all day. It was rumoured that the jury would take a long time to reach a verdict.

The trial was a source of great distress for Miss Manette and her father. Mr. Carton noticed that she was about to faint. He helped her out of the courtroom.

He returned to inform Mr. Lorry and the prisoner that she was feeling better. Mr. Carton's manner was careless and almost insolent.

Mr. Darnay thanked him for all his help but said that he expected the worst verdict.

An hour and a half passed slowly. Jerry rushed to the waiting group of Mr. Lorry, Miss Manette, Dr. Manette and Mr. Stryver. The verdict was 'Acquitted'.

Mr. Charles Darnay was released and his friends congratulated him on his escape from death.

Mr. Darnay kissed Miss Lucie Manette's hand gratefully. He then thanked Mr. Stryver.

Mr. Lorry said, "It has been a terrible day. We should all go home." He looked pointedly at Dr. Manette. His face had become frozen. The doctor looked carefully at Darnay with fear and distrust. His thoughts seemed to have wandered away.

"Father," said Lucie softly. "Shall we go home?"

He shook the shadow off and said, "Yes".

Mr. Lorry and Darnay were left on the pavement after the others departed. Mr. Carton joined them.

He had been standing in the shadows, leaning against a wall. Nobody had acknowledged his part in the day's proceedings as nobody had known of it.

Mr. Lorry found Mr. Carton's company disagreeable and he left too. Darnay thanked Carton for his help once again.

"I do not want any thanks," said Carton carelessly. "I don't know why I did it. I don't even particularly like you."

26

"You have acted as if you do," said Darnay.

"I care for no man on earth," said Carton, "and no man on earth cares for me. But there's a fair young lady who pitied you and wept for you. It must feel good to be the object of such sympathy and compassion."

Darnay did not react to this statement but wished him, and left.

Carton was left alone.

Mr. Stryver was a well-known lawyer with a large and lucrative practice. But he was not a very accomplished lawyer. Sidney Carton was the most unpromising of men but he was a great help to Stryver. Every night they would sit together and drink late through the night. Carton never had a case in hand but could extract the essence from the statements given by the witnesses. This assisted Stryver in preparing for his cases for the following day.

Dr. Manette lived in a quiet street corner of London. The front windows of his house had a pleasant view of the street which was lined by trees and wild flowers. The doctor occupied two floors of a large house. He received patients in this house and earned as much as he wanted.

His daughter made use of their little means to give an agreeable character to the house. She used her taste to give it a delightful effect.

Miss Pross had been with Miss Manette since she was ten years old and helped her in the house.

Mr. Lorry was a frequent visitor to the Manette home. One Sunday afternoon, four months after the trial for treason, he walked upto the house to dine with the doctor who had become his dear friend.

He was received by Miss Pross. Mr. Lorry was concerned for his friend, the Doctor. He asked Miss Pross, "Does the doctor refer to his shoe-making time, with Lucie?"

"Never," said Miss Pross, "but he still keeps the bench and tools with him."

"Does he talk of his being oppressed?" asked Mr. Lorry, "Or, mention the name of the person who caused him this pain?"

"I don't think he does," said Miss Pross, "but Miss Manette feels he often thinks about it. I think he is afraid of the whole subject."

"Afraid?"

"It's plain," said Miss Pross, "he may never feel certain that he may not lose himself again."

"True," said Mr. Lorry. "Yet, a doubt lurks in my mind, whether it is good for Dr. Manette to suppress his feelings and keep them shut up within him."

"It can't be helped," said Miss Pross. "If we touch that topic, he instantly changes for the worse."

As they were talking, Miss Lucie and Dr. Manette walked in and they all sat down for dinner.

After dinner they were joined by Mr. Darnay and Mr. Carton.

The conversation turned to the topic of the old buildings of London.

"Have you seen the Tower of London?" asked Mr. Darnay.

"Lucie and I have been there," said Dr. Manette.

"They told me a curious thing when I was there," said Darnay, talking of the day of his imprisonment.

"While making some alterations in an old dungeon in the tower, the workmen had to dig up the floor. Beneath a stone, they found a leather case. An old prisoner had written something on a paper and hidden it away to keep it from the jail."

Dr. Manette suddenly started up, with his hand on his head. He looked terrified. "Father," exclaimed Lucie, "are you ill?"

He recovered himself instantly. "No, my dear," he said.

Mr. Lorry detected a look of fear on the doctor's face. It was the same look he had seen earlier, after the trial.

Mr. Carton did not take part in the conversation but leaned against a window watching them.

THREE

Monsieur de Marquis

In Paris, Monsieur de Marquis was leaving for the Grand Opera. He was a man of about sixty, handsomely dressed and with a haughty gait. He got into his carriage and drove through the city. Common people rushed out of the horses' way. His driver drove as if he were charging an enemy.

The carriage dashed through streets and swept around corners. Women screamed before it and clutched each other and children ran out of its way. At last, at a street corner one of the wheels of the carriage came to a sickening little jolt. There was a loud cry from a crowd of people. The horses reared and stopped.

"What has gone wrong?" asked the Marquis, looking out of the window.

A tall man picked up a bundle lying near the feet of the horses and gave out a howl like a wild animal.

"Why does he make that abominable noise?" said the Marquis.

"It is a pity," said a man. "It's his child."

"Killed," shrieked the man, extending, both his arms above his head. "Dead!"

The people came closer, and looked at the Marquis. They did not say anything.

Monsieur de Marquis ran his eyes over them all, as if they were rats that had come out of their holes. He took out his purse.

"It is extraordinary to me," he said, "that you people cannot take care of yourselves and your children. How do I know what injury you have done to my horses? Give him this."

He threw out a gold coin towards his valet.

The man called out again with a most unearthy cry, "Dead!"

Another man joined the rest of the group. The miserable father of the child fell on his shoulder, sobbing and crying.

"I know all," said the man who had just come. "Be a brave man, Gaspard! It is better for the poor little child to die like this, than to live. He must have died in a moment without pain. Could he have lived an hour as happily?"

"You are a philosopher," said the Marquis smilingly. "What's your name?"

"Defarge. I sell wine," said the man.

The Marquis threw another gold coin and said, "Pick that up, philosopher, and spend it as you will. Are the horses alright?"

The Marquis leaned back in his seat and drove away as if he had accidently broken some common thing and had paid for it.

Suddenly a coin came flying into his carriage and fell on the floor.

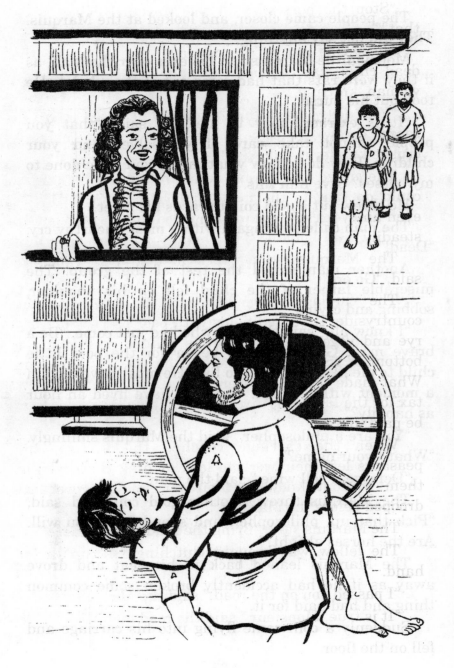

"Stop the horses," said the Marquis. "Who threw that?"

He looked out of the carriage. The father of the dead child was on the road and beside him stood a woman, knitting.

"You dogs," said the Marquis. "If I knew which rascal threw the coin at the carriage, he would be crushed under its wheels."

The crowd knew from experience that such a man could do that to them. No one raised their voice or even an eye. The woman who stood knitting looked up steadily.

The Marquis leaned back in his seat again and said, "Go on!"

The carriage drove through the city into the countryside. It passed fields with poor patches of corn, rye and vegetables. There was a little village at the bottom of a hill. The villagers there were very poor. What made them poor were taxes. Tax for the church, tax for the landlord, taxes to be paid here and taxes to be paid there.

When the carriage reached the village, the peasants left their work to look at him. He looked at them without knowing their misery. The peasants drooped before the Marquis.

The Marquis said, "Bring the road mender here!"

The fellow was brought clutching his cap in his hand.

"I passed you on the road," said the Marquis.

"It is true, Monsieur," said the road mender.

"What did you look at, so carefully?" said the Marquis.

The road mender stooped a little and pointed under the carriage. "I looked at the man who swung by the chain."

"Who?" demanded the Marquis, "Who was the man?"

"He did not belong to this part of the country, Monsieur," said the road mender. "I never saw him before. He jumped off and ran away.

The Marquis turned to the postmaster and told him to look for the man and then ordered his driver to move on.

His chateau was at the top of the hill. It was a large building with a long stone courtyard. Two stone staircases met in a stone terrace. Stone statues of men and stone heads of lions were kept in all directions. The chateau was more than two centuries old.

The Marquis entered the chateau and went straight to the dining room. The table was laid for two people.

"Has my nephew arrived?" he asked. He was told that he had not arrived but was expected.

The Marquis sat down to eat a sumptuous supper. He heard a sound from outside and asked his servant to check what was wrong. The servant opened the blinds of the window but saw nothing.

Half-way through the supper, his nephew arrived. It was none other than Charles Darnay. He had come from London.

34

The Marquis received him without shaking his hand. The uncle and nephew did not seem to see eye to eye.

After supper, Darnay told his uncle of the trial and his narrow escape from death.

The Marquis said, "Things in France have changed for the worse. Our ancestors had the right to send people to death, not long ago. We have lost many privileges because a new philosophy is gaining fame. Very bad, very bad!"

"I believe our family and its name was the most detested one in France," said Charles.

"For our family," said the Marquis, "it was a compliment. We must keep the dogs obedient with a whip."

"We have misused our position, both in the old times and in the present," said the nephew gloomily.

"I will do my best to preserve the honour of the family, if you will not," said the Marquis, getting up to leave.

"Our family has done a world of wrong by injuring every human creature who has come between us and our pleasures," said Charles. "You are my father's twin brother and have inherited his name and title after his death. I am bound to a system that is frightful to me. I must fulfill my mother's last request to have mercy and to redress the wrong that has been done by the family."

"I will never assist you on that account," said the Marquis.

"I renounce this property and France," said Charles.

"You may renounce France but not this property," said the Marquis.

"If it ever becomes mine," said Charles, "it shall be put into hands that will free it from the misery it has caused to people."

"And you," asked the uncle. "How will you live? In England?"

"Yes," said Charles.

"You have found a doctor with a daughter in England," said the Marquis.

"Yes," said Charles.

It would have been of no use to ask him how he knew of them.

"Good night!" said the uncle and left for his room.

The next morning, as the villagers woke up, they heard the ringing of the chateau's great bell.

All the people of the village gathered at the fountain, whispering in low voices, curious and surprised.

The Marquis had been stabbed in his bed. A knife was driven into his heart. A paper was attached to the knife, on which was written—

"Drive him fast to his tomb. This, from Jacques."

FOUR

The Proposal

More than a year had passed. Mr. Charles Darnay now lived in England as a tutor. He taught French to people as he was conversant with French literature.

Charles Darnay loved Lucie Manette dearly. He had loved her since his trial. He had never heard a sweeter voice, he had never seen a face more beautiful than hers. But, he never told her of his love for her. He wanted to tell Dr. Manette about his feelings before he spoke to her.

One summer day, he found the doctor alone at home. Lucie and Miss Pross were out.

Dr. Manette greeted Charles warmly.

"Dr. Manette," said Charles, "I know that Lucie has gone out. I take this opportunity to speak to you."

"Yes?" said the doctor. "Is Lucie the topic?"

"She is," said Charles hesitatingly. "I love your daughter dearly."

The doctor bent his eyes to the ground, "I have no doubt about your love for Lucie," he said. "Have you spoken to her about it?"

"No," said Charles. "I know that there is an unusual affection between you and Miss Manette. If I can make her my wife one day, I could never want to separate her and you. I would like to share your life and home and be faithful to you. Not take away your companion and friend."

The doctor looked up and asked, "Does Lucie love you?"

"I have no reason to believe that she does," said Charles, "Does she have any other suitor?"

"Mr. Carton and Mr. Stryver are here often," said Dr. Manette, "May be one of them or both are."

"I beg you to promise," said Charles, "if Miss Manette shows any interest in me, you will remember what I have said to you.

"I give you my promise," said the doctor.

"I must also tell you," continued Charles, "that my present name is slightly different from the name I am known by in France."

"Stop," said the doctor. "Tell me when I ask you, not now. If Lucie loves you and agrees to marry you, you shall tell me your name on your marriage morning."

"Willingly," said Charles, shaking his hand.

"God bless you!" said the doctor as Charles left.

It was dark when Lucie returned home.

She called out to her father but did not get an answer. She went to his door and heard a low hammering sound in his bedroom. Her blood chilled and she cried, "What shall I do!"

But, he soon came out of his room. They walked up and down for a long time.

That same night Mr. Stryver told Sidney of his intentions of asking Miss Manette to marry him.

"She is a charming creature," he said. "I am pretty well off and she will consider it her good fortune to marry me."

Carton made no comment.

"I want to have a word to you," said Stryver. "You are in a bad way. You don't know the value of money and one day you will be ill and poor. You should find somebody to take care of you. Marry some respectable woman with a little property."

"I'll think of it," said Sidney.

Mr. Stryver resolved to propose to Lucie before leaving for his vacation. He had no doubt that she would accept him. He met Mr. Lorry to tell him of his plans as he was very close to the Manettes.

"Oh dear me!" cried Mr. Lorry when he heard Mr. Stryver. "You are both eligible and prosperous but I would not advise you to propose without having some cause to believe that you will succeed."

"I beg your pardon!" said Stryver angrily.

"If you want, I will go to the Manettes and observe if my advice is sound or not," said Mr. Lorry.

"I will expect you this evening," said Stryver.

That evening Mr. Lorry called on Mr. Stryver late at night to confirm his opinion. "I was right this morning, Mr. Stryver. I have no doubt about it."

Mr. Stryver thanked him and said, "I am sorry that the young woman has committed this mistake. She will repent her decision."

Sidney Carton often visited the Manettes in their home. One day, in August, he went to meet Lucie. He found her alone doing her work. She was never quite at ease with him but she greeted him and invited him to sit near her table.

"You do not look well Mr. Carton," she commented.

"The life I lead Miss Manette, is not good for health," said Sidney.

Lucie was surprised to see tears in his eyes as he continued, "I want to say something to you. Will you hear me?"

"I would be glad to," said Lucie, "If it makes you feel any good."

"Don't be afraid of what I say. I love you and I know that it is impossible for you to return this love. I don't ask you to either. I have loved you since the day I first saw you. I know I am quite undeserving of your love."

Lucie was pale and trembling, "Can I not help you without returning your love?" she asked.

"I only wanted to open my heart to you," he said, "I want no more from you. I want to remember this day as the day I have shared my feelings with you. But, no one but you should ever know of them."

"Mr. Carton," said Lucie, a little agitated, "the secret is safe with me. I promise to respect it."

"Thank you, and God bless you," said Carton. "I will never refer to it again. But remember, I will do anything for you or for anyone dear to you. For you, I am ready to make any sacrifice."

"I will, Mr. Carton."

FIVE

The Knitting

In Paris, at noon time, two men in dusty clothes entered a wine-shop. Monsieur Defarge greeted them and introduced one of the men to his wife. "This man is called Jacques. He is a mender of roads. I met him by accident on his journey to Paris. Give him a drink."

After he had refreshed himself with a glass of wine. Monsieur Defarge took the road mender to the room that was once occupied by Dr. Manette. There were three men in the room. All of them were called Jacques.

Defarge closed the door and asked the road mender to tell the men his story.

"A year ago, I saw a man under the carriage of the Marquis. I had never seen him before but only noticed that he was very tall. The Marquis ordered his capture and he was captured after ten or eleven months. I was working on the hill-side and I saw him coming down the hill with six soldiers. His arms were bound—tightly to his sides and were swollen. His wooden shoes were large and clumsy, and so he walked slowly. The soldiers drove him forward by the butt-ends of their muskets. He fell down and the soldiers laughed. His face was bleeding and covered with dust. But, he could not wipe it. They took him to the village prison to lock him up. The villagers whispered to each other but said nothing. He remained in the prison for a few days but was not executed. The villagers said that petitions had been sent to the king saying that he had turned mad because of the death of his child."

"The petition was given to the king by Defarge," said one of the Jacques. "He did so at the risk of his own life by darting out before the horses of the King's carriage."

"Go on," said Defarge.

"The village said that the man was to be executed because he had killed the Marquis. On Sunday night, when the village was asleep, the soldiers raised a gallows forty feet high, by the fountain. They hung the prisoner there and left him hanging, poisoning the water. I left the village and met this comrade who brought me here."

"Good," said one of the Jacques, "Will you wait for us outside?"

"Willingly," said the road mender.

Left alone, Defarge said, "We will register this as doomed to destruction. Extermination to the chateau and all the race."

"Are you sure," asked Jacques, "that keeping the register will not cause us any embarrassment. Will she be able to decipher it?"

"Even if my wife was to keep the register in her memory, she would never lose a word of it. She has knitted it in her stitches and her own symbols. No one can erase one letter from her knitted register."

42

There was a murmur of confidence and approval among the men.

Monsieur Defarge went to leave the road mender to his village. When he returned, he told his wife that a spy called John Barsad had been commissioned to get information about them. He had been told this by his friends in the police. Defarge gave his wife the description of his appearance to help her recognise him.

The next day the spy came to the wine-shop. Madame Defarge observed him and continued her knitting. John Barsad was registered in her knitting.

The spy tried to strike a conversation with Madame Defarge. "A bad business this," he said, "the execution of Gaspard."

"If people use knives to kill," said Madame, coolly, "they have to pay for it."

"I believe there is much compassion and anger in this neighbourhood," said Barsad.

"Is there?" asked madame. "Here is my husband." The wine-shopkeeper entered the door. "Good day, Jacques," said the spy.

"You are mistaken, Monsieur," said Monsieur Defarge. "I am Earnest Defarge."

"It is all the same," said the spy. "I had the pleasure of chatting with Madame when you entered. There is much sympathy and anger for poor Gaspard here."

"I know nothing of it," said Defarge.

"I have the honour of knowing your old master Dr. Manette," said Barsad. "He was brought to you when he was released?"

"Certainly," said Defarge. "We have not heard from them since long."

"Miss Manette is going to be married." said the spy. "She is going to be married to the nephew of Monsieur the Marquis who is now the present Marquis. In England, he is not known by his family name but as Charles Darnay."

Madame Defarge kept knitting but this news had a significant effect on her husband. His hand was not steady as he lit his pipe. The spy did not fail to see this. Having made at least one hit, he departed.

"Can it be true?" said Defarge, in a low voice looking at his wife.

"If it is?" said his wife.

"If it is true," said Defarge. "I hope, for her sake, her husband stays out of France."

"Her husband's destiny will take him where he is to go," said Madame Defarge calmly. "I have registered both of them here. That is certain."

SIX

The Wedding

Lucie spent the last evening with her father before her marriage. They sat alone under a tree. "You are happy, my dear father?" she asked.

"Quite, my child," said Dr. Manette.

She put her arms around his neck and said, "Are you quite sure that my new duties will not come between us?"

"Quite sure, my darling!" said Mr. Manette more cheerfully than he felt. "My future seems brighter after your marriage than it ever was."

"If I had never seen Charles, my father," said Lucie. "I should have been quite happy with you." He embraced her and blessed her and thanked the Heavens for having bestowed her on him.

After their marriage, Lucie and Charles would occupy the upper rooms in the same building as Dr. Manette. They had supper together. They bid goodnight and separated for the night.

The marriage day was shining brightly. The beautiful bride, Mr. Lorry and Miss Pross were ready to go to the Church. Charles Darnay and Dr. Manette were together behind the closed door of the doctor's room.

45

When they came out of the room, Mr. Lorry noticed that the doctor was deadly pale but he looked composed and his manner was unaltered. He gave his arm to his daughter and took her downstairs. The rest followed in another carriage. Charles and Lucie were happily married.

The couple left for a short holiday. The parting was not easy but Dr. Manette tried to cheer Lucie and told Charles, "Take her. She is yours!"

When they were gone, Mr. Lorry noticed the same old scared lost look on Dr. Manette's face. As he wandered away into his room, Mr. Lorry told Miss Pross, "I think it's best not to speak to him just now, or disturb him. I will come back after a while and then we will take him for a ride into the country."

When he came back, he heard a low sound of knocking from the doctor's rooms.

"Good God!" he said. "What's that?"

Miss Pross looked terrified, "O dear me! All is lost," she cried. "He doesn't know me, and is making shoes again!"

Mr. Lorry went into the doctor's room. The bench was turned towards the light. The doctor was bent down making shoes.

"Dr. Manette. My dear friend!" said Mr. Lorry.

The doctor looked at him for a moment half inquiringly, half as if he was angry at being spoken to—and bent over his work again.

Nothing would induce him to speak. He kept working in silence. Mr. Lorry knew that this must be kept secret from Lucie and from all who knew him. He

made Miss Pross write to Lucie that the doctor had been called away on work. Mr. Lorry let it be known that the doctor was not well and required a few days of complete rest. He took leave from the bank and resolved to spend time with the doctor.

Miss Pross and he divided the night to keep watch over the doctor. In the day Mr. Lorry spoke to him on topics that had been familiar to them. He did not get any reply but it was clear that Dr. Manette thought about them.

The time went on very slowly and Mr. Lorry's heart grew heavier. The third day came and went, the fourth, the fifth. Five days, six days, seven days, eight days, nine days.

On the tenth morning, Mr. Lorry woke up and went to the doctor's room and looked in. The shoemaker's bench and tools were put aside and the doctor sat reading at the window. His face was calm though still very pale.

He advised Miss Pross that they should meet the doctor as if nothing unusual had occurred.

When breakfast was over, Mr. Lorry asked the doctor, "My dear Manette, I would like to have your opinion in confidence on a very curious case. It is about a very dear friend of mine. Please give me advise for his sake and above all for his daughter's."

"If I understand," said the doctor, "some mental shock...."

"Yes!"

"Be explicit," said the doctor. "Spare no details."

Mr. Lorry saw that he understood him and proceeded, "It is the case of an old and prolonged shock. He has recovered from the shock but unfortunately there has been a slight relapse."

"How long was the relapse?" asked the doctor.

"Nine days and nights," said Mr. Lorry. "It showed itself in the resumption of some old act."

"Did you speak of it to his daughter?"

"No. I kept it from her and will always keep it from her," said Mr. Lorry.

"That was very kind of you," said the doctor grasping his hand. "It was very thoughtful!"

"Now tell me, my dear Manette," said Mr. Lorry, "how does this relapse come about? Is there a danger of another? Can it be prevented? How should it be treated? What can I do for my friend?"

"I think your friend had foreseen the relapse," said the doctor. "He had dreaded it. I believe that there had been a strong revival of the cause of the problem. Some associations, of distressing nature was recalled. I have great hope for the future. He yielded under the pressure but I hope that the worst is over!"

"I am thankful!" said Mr. Lorry. He then came to the last point. "Should he keep the things associated with this occupation close to him?"

"I believe he is hopeful that he will never need them again," said the doctor.

"In short," said Mr. Lorry, "If the things were gone, might be the fear will go with it."

There was a silence.

"You see," said the doctor, "it is such an old companion."

"I would recommend him to sacrifice it," said Mr. Lorry, "Come! Give me your authority. For his daughter's sake!"

"In her name then let it be done," said the doctor. "But I would not take it away while he was present."

Mr. Lorry readily agreed. After three days the doctor went away to join Lucie and her husband.

On the night of the day on which he left the house, Mr. Lorry went into his room with a chopper, saw, chisel and hammer. He hacked the shoemaker's bench to pieces. Miss Pross burned the pieces in the kitchen fire. The tools, shoes and leather were buried in the garden.

When the newly-married pair came home, the first person who came to offer his congratulations was Sidney Carton. He took Charles Darnay aside and said, "Mr. Darnay, I wish we might be friends."

"We are already friends. I hope," said Charles.

"You remember a certain occasion," said Sidney, "when I was insufferable about liking you, and not liking you. I wish you would forget it."

"I forgot it long ago," said Charles.

They shook hands and Sidney went away.

When he was gone, Charles mentioned their conversation in the presence of Miss Pross, the doctor and Mr. Lorry.

His wife later told him, "I think poor Mr. Carton deserves more consideration and respect than you expressed for him tonight."

"I did not mean to do him any harm," said Charles.

"He may have his faults but he has a heart he very seldom reveals. There are deep wounds in it," said Lucie. "I am sure that he is capable of good and gentle things."

"I will always remember it, as long as I live," said Charles and took her in his arms.

Time passed and Lucie gave birth to a little girl. The sound of her tiny feet and sweet words filled the house. She also had a son who died when he was very small. Sidney Carton visited them a few times a year. He was the first stranger little Lucie became friends with.

Mr. Stryver married a widow with property and three boys. Stryver asked Charles to take the three boys as his pupils.

Lucie's little daughter was six years old when an awful sound like that of a great storm, began in France.

One day, in mid-July of the year, 1789, Mr. Lorry came from the bank. "There is such an uneasiness in Paris! Our customers seem to be in a hurry to send their properties to us in England. Thank God everything is safe and well here."

SEVEN

The Revolution

In Paris, a tremendous roar arose. A crowd clutching any weapon they could get hold of marched towards the Bastille.

Defarge led the men and his wife, holding an axe and a knife, led the women.

The attack began with alarm-bells ringing and drums beating. The draw bridge was lowered and after two fierce hours of fighting the fortress surrendered.

"The prisoners!"

"The records!"

"The secret cells!"

"The instruments of torture!"

"The prisoners!"

The sea of people rushed in, threatening the prison officers with instant death if any secret nook was left undisclosed.

"Show me the North Tower!" said Defarge. "Quick!"

"I will," said the official, "but there is no one there."

"What is the meaning of One Hundred and Five, North Tower?" asked Defarge.

"It is a cell, Monsieur."

"Show it to me!"

52

"This way."

They passed through gloomy vaults where the light of the day never shone. The three Jacques followed close behind. They passed doors of dark dens and cages down flights of steep steps. The jailor turned the key of one door and said, "One Hundred and Five, North Tower!"

There was a stool, table and a straw bed in the cell. The walls were blackened and a rusted iron ring hung from one of them. As they passed the torch on the walls, Defarge saw "A.M." on one of the walls.

"Alexander Manette," said Defarge, "And here he wrote, 'a poor physician'." He scratched a calendar on this stone. Jacques, take my knife and rip open that bed and search the straw."

He then crawled upon the hearth and peered up the chimney. Some dust came down. He groped it with caution.

"Nothing in the wood, nothing in the straw, Jacques. Nothing."

They retraced their way to the courtyard. The hour had come to execute the governor who had defended the Bastille. He could no longer hoist up men from lamps. The iron hand of tyranny and domination was down. As he dropped dead, Madame Defarge put her foot upon his neck, and with her cruel knife—cut off his head.

As the eight strong towers of the fortress were opened people discovered letters and other memorials of prisoners of earlier times, long dead of broken hearts.

A week later Madame Defarge sat in the wine-shop looking out at the street. Defarge came in breathless and looked around him.

"Listen, everyone!" said his wife, "What is the news?"

"Does everybody recall old Foulon, who told the famished people that they might eat grass, and who died?" asked Defarge.

"Everybody knows him!" shouted all those present.

"The news is about him," said Defarge. "He is not dead. He had a mock funeral as he feared us. But they found him alive, hiding in the country and brought him to Paris as a prisoner."

There was a moment of silence.

Defarge and his wife looked at each other and he said, "Patriots are we ready?"

Soon the drum was beating in the streets. People marched forward flinging their arms and shrieking, "Give us the head of Foulon. Give us the blood of Foulon. Give us the heart of Foulon. Give us the body and soul of Foulon. Tear him to pieces and dig him into the ground. Let grass grow from him!"

They reached the Hall of Examination where the old man, ugly and wrecked faced his trial.

"See!" cried Madame Defarge, pointing with her knife. "See the old villain bound with ropes."

The trial went on for two or three hours. Madame Defarge looked on impatiently. The crowd could no longer bear to wait. A cry rose through the hall, "Bring him out! Bring him to the lamp!"

Down and up he was pulled on to the steps of the building. Now on his knees; now on his feet, now on his back; dragged and struck at, stifled by the bunches of grass thrust into his face by hundreds of hands. Torn, bruised, panting, bleeding, beseeching for mercy, he was hauled to the nearest street corner where one of the fatal lamps swung. His head was soon on a pike and people danced at the sight.

When the day closed, his son-in-law, another of the people's enemies was brought to Paris. He too met with the same fate as Foulon.

There was a change in the villages too. The village where Monsieur de Marquis had been killed also felt the change. As the villages slept and the night deepened, the Chateau was set on fire. The fire grew higher, broader and brighter.

Some soldiers galloped to the gates of the chateau. A group of officers stood looking at the fire. "Help, gentlemen—officers!—The chateau is on fire! Valuable objects may be saved from the flames by timely aid! Help! Help!"

The officers gave no orders; and answered, "It must burn."

The chateau was left to burn itself.

Monsieur Gabelle who was the chief functionary of the place hid in his house for the night. The next morning he came out. His life was spared but he was taken as a prisoner.

EIGHT

Return to Paris

In August of the year 1792, the Tellson's Bank in London was a great gathering-place for many Marquis of France. Those nobles who had seen the coming storm in time, and anticipating plunder or confiscation, had sent their money to the Tellson's. So every newcomer from France first visited the Tellson's.

Mr. Lorry was preparing to visit France. A lot of papers and books of the bank were still in France. He feared that if any documents were seized or destroyed it would make their business transaction very difficult.

Charles Darnay tried to dissuade him from going as he was concerned for his safety but Mr. Lorry had made up his mind. "It is safe enough for me. Nobody will care to interfere with an old fellow like me," said Mr. Lorry. "I know the city and the business there better than anyone else."

"I admire the gallantry of your youthful spirit Mr. Lorry, "said Charles. "Do you really leave tonight?"

"I cannot delay it any further," said Mr. Lorry. "I will take Jerry with me."

They were talking at Mr. Lorry's desk at the bank. On the table there was a soiled and unopened letter. A bank clerk asked Mr. Lorry if he had traced the person to whom the letter was addressed. On the letter was written, "Very pressing. To Monsieur de Marquis St. Evrémonde of France."

Mr. Lorry said, "The gentleman has not been found. He is the nephew of the Marquis who was murdered. He did not agree with his uncle and abandoned the estates when he inherited them."

Charles could not stop himself any longer and said, "I know the fellow. I will take the letter to him."

When he was away from the bank, Charles opened the letter and read it. The letter was written from a prison in Paris by Gabelle. He wrote that he would soon be summoned before a tribunal and was sure to lose his life on charges of treason against the people. He asked Charles to help him as he had only acted for the people and not against them as commanded by Charles. He wrote that only Charles could save him and begged him to help to release him.

Charles felt very uneasy on reading the letter of an old and good servant. But he had not oppressed nor imprisoned any man. He had given Monsieur Gabelle written instructions to spare the people from payment and give them what little there was to give. He had proof that would help Gabelle and ensure his own safety.

Charles Darnay resolved that he would go to Paris. He met Mr. Lorry, on the night of his departure to Paris, and told him, "I have delivered that letter. There is no written answer but perhaps you will take a verbal one. There is a prisoner in Paris whose name is Gabelle. Simply tell him, 'He will come.'"

The next night Charles left for Paris. He left a letter for Lucie to be delivered to her after he had gone. He wanted to spare her the pain of separation. He also left a letter for Dr. Manette leaving his wife and child in his care.

When he reached France, Charles realised that there was no hope for him to return to England till he was declared a good citizen in Paris. Every town gate had a band of citizen-patriots who stopped all comers and goers, cross-questioned them, inspected their papers and looked for their names in their lists. They either turned them back, sent them to Paris or arrested them.

In a small inn where Charles was resting for the night, he was awakened by three armed patriots in red caps.

"We are going to send you to Paris," said one, "with an escort—and you must pay for it."

"Citizen," said Charles, "I want nothing more than to get to Paris but I do not need an escort."

"Silence!" growled a red-cap patriot. "You are an aristocrat and must have an escort."

"I have no choice," said Charles.

They travelled through the wet streets through the day and night, resting for short periods.

When they came to the town of Beauvais, a crowd gathered to see him. Many voices called out "Down with the emigrant!"

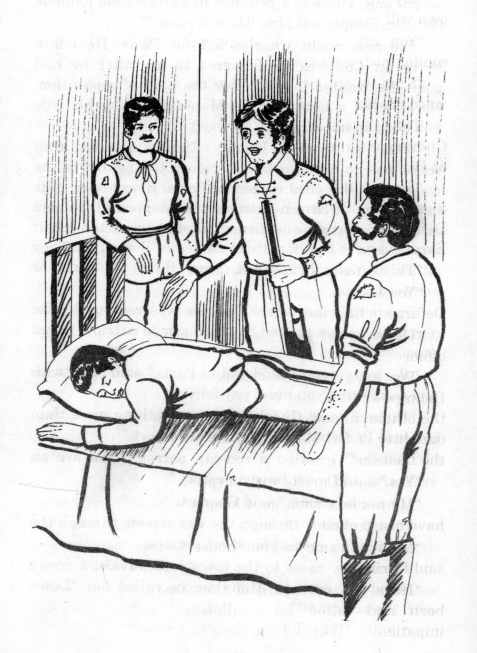

"My friend," said Charles, "I am in France of my own will."

"You are a cursed aristocrat!" they cried, "and condemned as a traitor."

"I am no traitor," said Charles, trying to make his voice heard.

The postmaster interposed himself between Charles and the crowd, "Let him be! He will be judged at Paris."

The next day they walked to Paris. He was taken to a guard-room where he was handed to a man, "Citizen Defarge," said the guard, "Is this the emigrant Evrémonde?"

"This is the man," said Defarge.

"You are consigned to the prison of La Force," said Defarge to Charles.

"Under what law?" asked Charles. "What is my offence?"

"We have new laws since you were here," said Defarge and led him on. When they were away from the others, he asked Charles, "Are you married to the daughter of Dr. Manette, who was once a prisoner in the Bastille?"

"Yes," said Darnay with surprise.

"My name is Defarge. I keep a wine-shop. You may have heard of me."

"My wife came to your house to take her father," said Darnay.

"Have you not heard of that sharp female newly born and called La Guillotine?" asked Defarge impatiently. "Why did you come to France?"

"I came voluntarily to help a fellow countryman," said Charles. "Do you not believe it is the truth? Will you help me?"

"No," said Defarge, looking straight ahead. "Other people have been similarly buried in worse prisons, before now."

"But never by me, Citizen Defarge," said Charles. "Can you inform Mr. Lorry of Tellson's Bank, an English gentleman who is now in Paris that I have been thrown into the prison of La Force?"

"I will do nothing for you," said Defarge doggedly.

When they reached the prison, Charles was led to a solitary cell which was cold and damp. There was a chair, a table and a straw mattress in the cell. Charles asked for some pen, ink and paper but was refused.

He walked to and fro in his cell, counting its measurements. "Five paces by four and a half, five paces by four and a half, five paces by four and a half."

NINE

Saving Charles

Mr. Lorry occupied the rooms in the bank. Looking out of his window, he said, "Thank God that no one near and dear to me is in this dreadful town tonight."

Soon afterwards, the great gate of the bank rang and his door suddenly opened. Two figures rushed in and Mr. Lorry fell back in amazement.

Lucie and her father!

"What is this?" cried Mr. Lorry. "What has happened? What has brought you here?"

"Charles," cried Lucie. "My husband! Is here in Paris. He is in the prison of La Force."

The old man uttered a cry. Just then they heard voices from the courtyard outside.

The doctor turned towards the window. Mr. Lorry led Lucie to another room. "Don't be terrified, my love," he said. "I know that, no harm has come to Charles."

When he returned to the window he whispered, "They are murdering the prisoners."

Dr. Manette hastened out of the room and was in the courtyard in the heart of the crowd. There was a pause when he said something softly. Then there were cries, 'Live the Bastille prisoner. Help for the Bastille prisoner's kindred in La Force. Save the prisoner Evrémonde at La Force.'

Lucie had, by that time fallen on the floor. Miss Pross had laid the child, who had also come, on the bed.

The next day Mr. Lorry shifted Lucie, her child and Miss Pross to a hired lodging near the bank. He left Jerry with them. The doctor had not returned and Mr. Lorry returned to the bank.

That night a strongly-made man with dark curly hair visited him. He was Monsieur Defarge and had a message from Dr. Manette. He handed him a scrap of paper on which a few words were written in the doctor's writing. "Charles is safe. I cannot leave this place yet. The bearer has a note from Charles to his wife. Let him see her."

In the courtyard there were two women, one was knitting. Mr. Lorry led them to Lucie's new lodgings. Mr. Lorry was struck by Defarge's manner. He spoke little and mechanically.

In his letter, Charles assured Lucie that he was well. Lucie was so relieved to hear from her husband that she kissed one of the hands that knitted but Madame Defarge made no response. Lucie looked at her face terrified and held her child to her breast.

"It is enough, my husband," said Madame Defarge. "I have seen them. We may go."

There was no visible menace in her manner but it was enough to alarm Lucie. She laid an appealing hand on Madame Defarge's dress.

"You will be good to my poor husband," she said. "For my sake and for my child's sake. As a wife and mother!"

Madame Defarge looked coldly at her and said, "Your husband is not my business. The wives and mothers we have been used to seeing since we were children were never considered. We have seen them suffer when their husbands and fathers laid in prison."

"We have seen nothing else," said the woman with her.

Madame Defarge resumed her knitting and they went out.

"Courage my dear Lucie," said Mr. Lorry but in his mind he was greatly troubled.

Dr. Manette returned on the fourth day. Eleven hundred defenceless prisoners of both sexes and all ages had been killed in four days and nights.

In the prison, a self-appointed Tribunal was sitting. Prisoners were brought before it and they were rapidly ordered to be massacred or to be released or sent back to their cells.

Dr. Manette had announced himself by name and profession and having been an unaccused prisoner in Bastille for eighteen years.

He ascertained that his son-in-law was among the living prisoners. Charles was brought before the Tribunal to be examined but the doctor could not have him released. He obtained the permission to remain in the prison as a physician. He was soon the inspecting doctor for three prisons, among them was La Force. He ensured that Charles was no longer confined alone but mixed with the other prisoners. He saw him weekly and brought messages to Lucie from him.

The king and his wife were tried and beheaded. The Republic of Liberty, Equality, Fraternity or Death declared its victory. The Guillotine became a popular figure. Models of it were worn on the necks in place of the cross.

One year and three months passed, but the doctor was confident that he would get Charles released. He used his profession to make himself indispensable in the hospital and the prison. He was a man apart for both assassins and victims. The story of the Bastille captive made him above all other men. He was not suspected or questioned.

During all that time Lucie was never sure when the Guillotine would strike off her husband's head. Her father tried to reassure her, "Nothing can happen to him without my knowledge. I know I can save him."

Lucie used to wait for Charles in the street near the prison. Dr. Manette had told her, "If you stood in a certain place in the street, Charles can sometimes see you from the upper window in the prison. He can get to it at three in the afternoon. But you will not be able to see him."

In all weathers, she waited there two hours. Sometimes she would take her child with her.

Her husband saw her once out of five or six times but she could never see him.

After many months, she was informed by her father that Charles would face his trial the next day.

The Tribunal consisted of five judges, public prosecutor and a jury.

"Charles Evrémonde, called Darnay!"

When his name was called, Charles stepped forward. Fifteen prisoners had been tried before him. All the fifteen had been condemned.

Among the audience sat Defarge and his wife. Dr. Manette and Mr. Lorry were also present.

Charles was accused as an emigrant. Under the new law all emigrants were to be put to death.

"Take off his head!" cried the audience. "An enemy to the Republic!"

The prosecutor asked the prisoner if it was not true that he had lived in England for many years.

Charles agreed but said that he had relinquished his title and lived by his own earnings and not on the money from the estate. He named Dr. Manette and Gabelle as his witnesses. He had married a citizeness of France who was the daughter of Dr. Manette.

This had a happy effect on the audience as the doctor was well known. Those who had been ready to kill him a moment ago were now moved, some to tears.

Charles continued, he had returned to France to help a fellow citizen's life. He presented Gabelle's letter as proof. Gabelle confirmed it as he had been set free from prison a few days ago.

Dr. Manette was questioned next. He told the jury that Charles had actually been tried in England as an enemy of that country. Mr. Lorry was presented as a witness in that trial.

The jury voted in Charles' defence and the prosecutor declared him free. The audience shouted in the prisoner's favour. This showed their fickleness. No sooner was he acquitted, tears were shed and the prisoner was embraced. They all shouted, "Long live the Republic!"

They put him on a chair and carried him to his home on men's shoulders.

Lucie fell into her father's arms on hearing the news.

"Oh dearest Charles, let me thank God for this," she cried as Charles took his wife in his arms.

"Now thank your father," said Charles, "No other man in all France could have done what he has done for me."

Dr. Manette said, "I have saved him."

TEN

A Knock on the Door

Miss Pross and Jerry decided to go and shop for some provisions for the house. They left Lucie and her husband, father and child near bright fire. Mr. Lorry was expected back presently.

All was quiet and Lucie felt more at ease than she had been for many months.

Just then there was knock on the door.

"Oh father!" cried Lucie. "What can this be. Hide Charles. Save him."

"I have saved him," said the doctor. "Let me go to the door."

Four armed men in red caps, entered the room.

"Charles Evrémonde, you are again the prisoner of the Republic," they said, surrounding him.

"What is he accused of?" asked the doctor.

"It is against the rule," answered one of the men. "Ask no questions."

"But who has accused him?"

"Citizen and citizeness Defarge and by one other."

"What other?"

"You will be answered tomorrow," said the man and looked at the doctor with a strange look.

70

Unconscious of the new calamity at home, Miss Pross and Jerry went to a wine-shop to buy some wine. Two men sat in a corner of the shop. When one of them got up to leave, he came face to face with Miss Pross. She let out a scream and clapped her hands.

"Oh Solomon," she cried, recognising her brother who had been missing for a long time. A few years ago Solomon had spent all her money never to return.

Solomon told her to be quiet and quickly led her to a dark corner of the street.

"Don't call me Solomon. Do you want me dead?" he said in a frightened voice. "What do you want?"

"How unkind of you to show me no affection," cried Miss Pross.

Jerry who had been quiet, touched his shoulder and said, "I know you. You were a witness in Mr. Charles Darnay's trial in England. What is your name?"

"Barsad," said another voice and Sidney Carton stepped forward from the shadows. "I arrived yesterday evening and went to Mr. Lorry. I saw Mr. Barsad coming out of the prison of the Conciergerie and followed you to the wine-shop. I overheard your conversation. Will you accompany me to the Tellson's Bank?"

"Are you threatening me?"

"I have a proposal to make for you that will be for our mutual satisfaction," said Sidney.

Barsad agreed to accompany him. They left Miss Pross at the corner of the street of her home.

Sidney took Barsad to Mr. Lorry at the bank. "I

have bad news," said Sidney, "Darnay has been arrested again."

"I left him safe and free two hours ago," exclaimed Mr. Lorry.

"I heard it from Mr. Barsad's conversation at the wine-shop," said Sidney. He then turned to Barsad and said, "I know that you are a spy for the republican French government but formerly you had worked for the aristocratic English government the enemy of France and freedom. I can take you to the nearest section committee and hand you to them, if you don't help us."

He saw that the spy was fearful. He had been thrown out of his employment in England and had accepted service in France.

"Who was your friend at the wine-shop?" asked Sidney, "he said he now works at the country-prisons."

"You don't know him," said Barsad quickly.

"Cly!" cried Carton. "He had disguised himself but he is the same man who had been at Charles' trial."

"Now come to the point," said Barsad, at last. "I have to go on duty soon. What is your proposal?"

"You are a jailor at the Conciergerie," said Sidney, "so you can come in and out when you choose."

"Yes."

"Come to the dark room and I want to talk to you alone," said Sidney leading him to another room.

Sidney spoke to Barsad in a low tone and Mr. Lorry and Jerry could not hear what was said. When they came out of the room Sidney led him out.

72

Mr. Lorry asked Sidney what he had done.

"Not much," said Sidney. "If things go wrong for Charles, I have insured that we can meet him once. Please don't tell Lucie of this meeting or this arrangement. It may add to her trouble. I shall be in the court tomorrow but only as one of the crowd."

Mr. Lorry went to the doctor's lodgings and Sidney went only till the gate. He then walked to a chemist's shop and gave him a list.

The chemist whistled softly as he read it. He made small packets and gave them to Sidney.

He put them, one by one, in his inner coat. "There in nothing to do until tomorrow," he said.

The next day the court was all astir and abuzz. Sidney stood in a corner and saw Mr. Lorry, Dr. Manette and Lucie sitting beside them.

When her husband was brought in, Lucie looked upon him with admiration, love and pity. She tried her best to be brave.

The same people presided over the Tribunal. The prosecutor asked the names of those who denounced the accused. They were Defarge, his wife and Alexandre Manette.

A great uproar took place in the court. Dr. Manette stood in his place looking pale and trembling.

"I protest," he cried. "You know the accused is the husband of my daughter, who is dearer to me than my life. Who says I denounce the husband of my child?"

"Citizen Manette, be calm," said the prosecutor. "If the Republic demands you to sacrifice your child, it is your duty to do so. Listen to what is to follow."

Defarge was produced before the court. He said that he had worked for the doctor as a boy and the doctor had been delivered to him when he was released from the prison. He looked at his wife and said that when the Bastille had been taken, he had found a paper in a hole in the chimney of the cell where Dr. Manette had been kept. The paper had the writing of Dr. Manette on it.

"Let it be read."

There was silence and stillness in the court as the paper was read.

ELEVEN

The Story is Retold

"I, Alexandre Manette am a physician and a resident of Paris. I am writing this from my cell in the last month of the year 1767. I am writing this with great difficulty using a rusty iron point and the soot and charcoal from the chimney mixed with blood. It is the tenth year of my captivity and I am in possession of my right mind and my memory is exact. I know my reason will not remain unimpaired for long.

In December 1957, as I was walking on a street near my residence, a carriage stopped next to me. There were two men in the carriage, wrapped in cloaks to conceal themselves. They were both about my age.

One of them asked me my name and asked me to enter the carriage when I identified myself.

I could do nothing but comply and the carriage drove on at a high speed. We left the streets of Paris and entered the country. We stopped at a solitary house. One of the young men slapped the man who opened the door, across the face, for not opening the door immediately. I than realised that the two men were twin brothers. I will call one of them elder because he exercised more authority than the one I will refer to as the younger brother.

I heard cries from the upper room. There was a patient with high brain fever, lying on a bed. She was a beautiful woman less than twenty years old. Her arms were tied to her sides. Her eyes were dilated and wild. She kept shrieking "My husband, my father and my brother!" and then counted upto twelve and said "Hush!" She would then pause and begin again.

I asked how long this had lasted.

"Since last night," said the elder brother.

They told me that there was a case of medicines in the closet. I made the patient swallow some with great difficulty.

I sat by her bed to watch over her. There was a timid woman in a corner who attended over her. She was the wife of the servant downstairs. There was no effect of the medicines upon the patient's cries.

The elder brother told me there was another patient. He took me to a back room. There was some hay on the ground on which a handsome peasant boy, about seventeen years old, was lying down. I could see that he was dying of a sword wound.

"I am a doctor," I said, "Let me examine you."

"Let it be," he answered.

"He is a crazy, common dog," said the elder brother. "He forced my brother to hurt him."

There was no pity or sorrow in his voice.

"Doctor, these nobles are very proud," said the boy, "but we common dogs are proud too. How is my sister? The other brother asked my sister's husband to lend her to him because he admired her. But, my sister was

good and virtuous and hated his brother. They made her husband work out in the cold with no food. He sobbed twelve times, once for every stroke of the bell and then died in her arms."

The boy was dying but gathered all his strength to tell his story.

"His brother then took my sister away for his pleasure," continued the boy. "I told my father but he could not do anything. I took my younger sister to a place beyond their reach so that she would be safe. I then tracked them here and climbed in from the window. He tossed me some money but I hit him and he thrust his sword in me. Lift me up doctor. Where is he?"

"He is here," I said and supported the boy.

"Marquis," said the boy. "You and your race will have to answer for this." He put his hand to the wound and drew a cross in the air with his forefinger. He then dropped down dead.

When I returned to his sister, I repeated the medicines but she never stopped her shrieks.

"What strength there is in these common bodies!" said the elder brother.

"There is strength in sorrow and despair," I said.

"Doctor, the things that you see here are not to be spoken of," said the Marquis.

The young girl lingered for a week. I tried to ask her of her family name but she kept her secret and died two hours before midnight.

"At last she is dead," said the Marquis, "I congratulate you, my brother."

He offered me money but I left it on the table. We parted without another word.

When I returned home, I wrote a letter to the Minister telling him of the two cases. I kept the matter a secret even from my wife.

The next day a lady visited me. She was the wife of the elder brother—the Marquis St. Evrémonde. She had discovered her husband's share in the cruel story and wanted to help the younger sister of the dead girl. She was a good and compassionate lady and not happy in her marriage. I could not help her as I knew nothing of the sister, so she left. There was a boy of two or three years with her. His name was Charles.

That night, a man in a black dress rang my bell and asked me to come for an urgent case. When I came out of the house, my mouth was covered. I saw the two brothers in a dark corner of the road. The Marquis took out the letter I had written to the minister and burnt it and then crushed it under his foot. Then I was brought here to my living grave.

I believe that the mark of the red cross is fatal to them and they will never get God's mercy. I, Alexandre Manette, denounce them and their descendants to Heaven and to Earth."

TWELVE

No Hope

A terrible sound arose when the reading of this document ended. The Defarges had made the paper public, bidding their time. This detested family name had long been knitted in the fatal register.

Madame Defarge was smiling, she murmured, "Save him now, my doctor, save him!"

The vote was unanimous, "Death within twenty four hours."

Lucie stood stretching out her arms towards her husband. "Let me touch him!" she cried, "If I might embrace him once!"

"Farewell my darling," said Charles, "Say farewell to our child."

Dr. Manette had followed her. Darnay put out a hand to him and said, "I know now, what you underwent. Heaven be with you!"

Charles was drawn away. Sidney came from an obscure corner and helped Lucie out of the door to the carriage. They drove back to their lodgings.

Little Lucie ran to Sidney and threw her arms round him, "Oh Carton," she cried, "Now that you have come, I think you will do something to help mamma, something to save papa."

He bent over the child and murmured some words in her ears, "A life you love." She was to remember these words till she was a handsome old lady.

Carton turned to Dr. Manette and told him to do what he could to help Charles. He asked the doctor to meet him at Mr. Lorry's at night.

Mr. Lorry led him to the door and said quietly, "I have no hope."

"Nor have I," said Sidney.

He went to Defarges. Madame Defarge cast a careless glance at him and then a keener and then a keener, and then went to him to ask him what he had ordered.

Sidney spoke to her in a strong English accent as he asked for some wine.

He heard her say to Defarge and Jacques Three, "I swear to you .... like Evrémonde!"

Defarge brought him the wine and to look at him. "Certainly a little like him," he said to his wife.

Sidney overheard Madame Defarge tell the others that she was the sister of the young girl and boy killed by the Evrémonde brothers. She now wanted to ensure that Lucie and her child would also meet the same fate as Charles. Under the new law, it was a capital crime to mourn for, sympathise with, a victim of the guillotine.

Sidney went to Mr. Lorry's room and found Dr. Manette had once again fallen back to his old mental state, "Where is my bench? What have they done with my work? I must finish those shoes."

Mr. Lorry and Sidney tried to smooth him and made him sit by the fire.

Sidney gave Mr. Lorry some papers and said, "This is the certificate which enables me to pass out of this city. Keep it for me. I will go to see Charles and I better not take it to the prison. Take this paper too, it is a certificate to ensure that the doctor, his daughter and her child would pass the barrier. Their life is in danger too. Madame Defarge plans to denounce them. The moment I come, drive away. All the arrangements must be made before that Lucie may not want to leave but tell her that it was her husband's last wish. Remember, any delay may cause the loss of many lives."

THIRTEEN

Fifty Two

In the black prison, fifty-two prisoners awaited their fate. Charles Darnay was alone in his cell. He knew that nothing could possibly save him. He was allowed to purchase some writing material.

He wrote a long letter to Lucie, a letter to her father and one to Mr. Lorry. He never thought of Carton.

He heard the door of his cell being unlocked. There stood Sidney Carton.

"I cannot believe it is you," said Charles. "Are you a prisoner?"

"I have been sent by your wife," said Sidney, "Quick! Change your clothes for mine."

"It is madness," said Charles, "We cannot escape from this place. You will only die with me."

"Do as I ask you Darnay," said Sidney. "Take this pen and ink and write what I shall dictate."

"To whom do I address it?"

"To no one. Write on—If you remember the words that passed between us, long ago. I am thankful that the time has come when I can prove them. I do it with no regret or grief. If it had been otherwise, I should have had so much more to answer for."

As he wrote, Carton's hand closed over Charles' nostrils and he fell down on the ground unconscious.

Quickly, Carton dressed himself in the prisoner's clothes and called Barsad who was waiting outside.

"He is the man I have exchanged. Take him with you out of the gate. Tell the guards that the parting with his friend has overpowered him. Take him to Mr. Lorry."

The door closed and Carton was left alone. He waited as the clock struck two. A jailor entered and ordered him to follow him. They went to a large dark room. A young woman with large eyes and a pale face came upto him, "Citizen Evrémonde," she said, "I am the poor little seamstress, who was with you in La Force."

"True," he murmured, "I forget what you were accused of."

"I was accused of plotting against the Republic," she said, "Heaven knows I am innocent."

His heart was warmed and softened to this pitiable girl. He pressed her fingers to his lips.

As her eyes lifted to his face, he saw a sudden doubt in them, "Are you dying for him?" she whispered.

"And his wife and child," said Sidney.

"Will you let me hold your brave hand, stranger?" she asked.

"Yes, my poor sister, to the last."

At the same hour, a coach going out of Paris was being examined.

Mr. Lorry showed the papers and identified the

travellers—Sidney Carton who was unconscious, Lucie, her daughter and Dr. Manette who was murmuring something to himself.

"How many did they say?" asked someone.

"I do not understand you," said Mr. Lorry.

"How many to the guillotine today?"

"Fifty-two."

"The guillotine goes handsomely. I love it. Move forward."

At the same time Madame Defarge was plotting with Jacques Three and her friend. She did not trust her husband as he had a weakness for the doctor and his family.

She had a witness who was prepared to testify that he had seen Lucie signalling to someone in the prison. She told her friend and Jacques to keep a seat for her to see the execution. She herself would go to Lucie.

"She will be at home waiting for her husband's death. She will be mourning and grieving and will speak against the republic and in favour of its enemies. I will go to her," she said.

It was nothing to her that an innocent man was to die for the sins of his forefathers. It was hopeless to appeal to her. Her hatred of a class had made her into a tigress without pity.

As Madame Defarge drew nearer and nearer to Lucie's home, Miss Pross and Jerry were planning their departure. They had not travelled with the others to avoid overloading the coach. Miss Pross told Jerry to bring a vehicle and pick her up from the

cathedral. Two carriages leaving the house on the same day might awaken suspicion.

Jerry was doubtful about leaving her alone but Miss Pross assured him that she would be safe.

When Miss Pross was alone, Madame Defarge entered the house. Miss Pross rocoiled at her sight.

"Where is the wife of Evrémonde," asked Madame Defarge. Then she raised her voice and called out, "Citizen doctor! Wife of Evrémonde! Child of Evrémonde!"

The following silence suggested that they were gone.

"They can be pursued and brought back," she said and turned to the door.

Miss Pross seized her round the waist in both her arms and held her tight. Madame Defarge hit her back and a fierce struggle followed.

Madame Defarge took out a loaded pistol, which lay hidden in her dress. Miss Pross saw it and struck at it. There was a flash and a crash.

Miss Pross stood alone blinded with smoke. The furious woman lay lifeless on the ground.

Miss Pross gathered her things and hurried out of the house, not before locking the door. She threw the key in the river on her way and finally met Jerry at the cathedral.

She asked him a question but could not hear his reply. "I don't hear you," she said.

And she never heard anything else in the world.

FOURTEEN

Peace

Sidney held the girl's hand while they were being driven on the cart.

"I think you were sent to me by Heaven," she said.

"Or you to me," said Sidney.

Madame Defarge's friends looked about for her, "She has never missed before," said one of the knitting women.

The girl was led to the guillotine before Sidney.

That evening they said that it was the most peaceful man's face ever seen there. If he had spoken before his end, he would have said, "I see Barsad, Defarge, the judge and the jury as the new oppressors taking the place of the old. I see the lives for which I lay down my life, peaceful, useful, prosperous and happy.

It is a far, far better thing that I do than I have ever done. It is a far, far better rest that I go to, than I have ever known."

Word-Meanings

summit	:	peak
emaciated	:	lean
inquiry	:	question
prevalent	:	existent
peril	:	danger
beckoned	:	made silent signal
solitude	:	single
summoned	:	called for
coherently	:	making sense
treason	:	treachery, offence of attempting to overthrow the government
grave	:	serious
warped	:	become twisted
lucrative	:	yielding profit
haughty	:	proud, vain
abominable	:	detestable
valet	:	a gentleman's personal servant
chateau	:	country house
sumptuous	:	lavish

ancestors	:	forefathers
redress	:	set right
renounce	:	give up
conversant	:	familiar with
muskets	:	guns
gallows	:	structure for hanging criminals
decipher	:	make out the meaning of
bestowed	:	gave
explicit	:	in detail
relapse	:	fall back
resumption	:	resumed
insufferable	:	unbearable
emigrant	:	person who has settled in another country
doggedly	:	persistently
massacred	:	indiscriminate killing
indispensable	:	necessary
relinquished	:	gave up
denounced	:	accused
dilated	:	opened wide
virtuous	:	morally good
unanimous	:	of one mind
recoiled	:	rebound
oppressors	:	who govern with tyranny

Questions

1. What was the state of England and France at the start of the story?
2. Why was a guard going along the coach?
3. Describe Dr. Manette when his daughter first saw him.
4. Five years later which case was under trial in England?
5. How did Sidney Carton prove the accused innocent?
6. Describe Monsieur de Marquis.
7. How did he react when his carriage killed the child?
8. Why did the Marquis and his nephew argue?
9. Who do you think killed the Marquis?
10. What did Charles Darnay do in England?
11. Why was Madame Defarge always knitting?
12. What do you think Charles Darnay told Dr. Manette before his marriage?
13. What was Defarge looking for in the cell of the Bastille?
14. What was the guillotine?
15. Why did Mr. Lorry need to visit Paris?

16. Why did Charles Darnay decide to go to Paris?

17. Why was Charles arrested when he reached Paris?

18. How was Charles released in the first trial in Paris?

19. Who was Solomon?

20. On whose accusation was Charles arrested the second time?

21. Who was responsible for the arrest of Dr. Manette?

22. Why did Dr. Manette write his letter ten years after his arrest?

23. Who were his two patients before his arrest?

24. Why did the girl shout, "My husband, my father and my brother?"

25. What was the significance of counting till twelve?

26. How did the doctor finally get arrested?

27. Describe how Madame Defarge planned to get Lucie and her child arrested?

28. How did Sidney save Charles?

29. How did Miss Pross lose her sense of hearing?

30. Why was Sidney at peace when he died?